D1389522

100
Hugs

Books by Chris Riddell

100 Hugs

Chris Riddell's Doodle a Day

Ottoline and the Yellow Cat
Ottoline Goes to School
Ottoline at Sea
Ottoline and the Purple Fox

Goth Girl and the Ghost of a Mouse
Goth Girl and the Fete Worse Than Death
Goth Girl and the Wuthering Fright

100
HUGS Chris Riddell

MACMILLAN CHILDREN'S BOOKS

First published 2017 by Macmillan Children's Books
an imprint of Pan Macmillan
20 New Wharf Road, London N1 9RR
Associated companies throughout the world
www.panmacmillan.com

ISBN 978-1-5098-1430-5

1 3 5 7 9 8 6 4 2

A CIP catalogue record for this book is available from
the British Library.

Printed and bound by CPI Group (UK) Ltd, Croydon CR0 4YY

ONE WORD FREES US OF ALL
THE WEIGHT AND PAIN OF LIFE:
THAT WORD IS LOVE.

SOPHOCLES

WORDS ARE EASY, LIKE THE WIND;
FAITHFUL FRIENDS ARE HARD
TO FIND.

WILLIAM SHAKESPEARE

I WOULD ALWAYS RATHER BE
HAPPY THAN DIGNIFIED.

CHARLOTTE BRONTË

HE'S MORE MYSELF THAN I AM.
WHATEVER OUR SOULS ARE MADE OF,
HIS AND MINE ARE THE SAME.

EMILY BRONTË

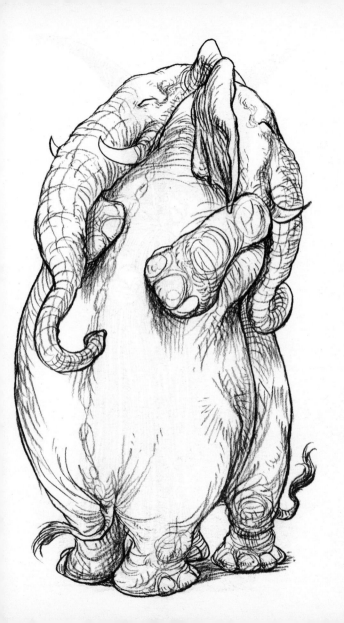

IF I HAD A FLOWER FOR EVERY TIME
I THOUGHT OF YOU...
I COULD WALK THROUGH MY GARDEN
        FOREVER.

                ALFRED, LORD TENNYSON

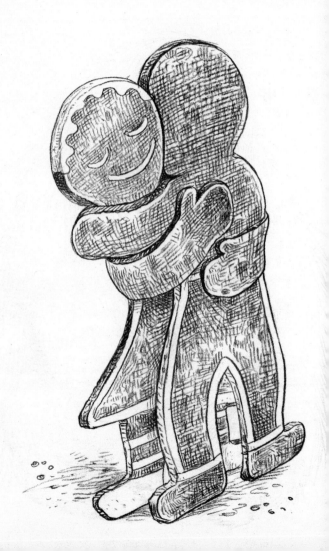

BEING DEEPLY LOVED BY SOMEONE
GIVES YOU STRENGTH, WHILE LOVING
SOMEONE DEEPLY GIVES YOU
COURAGE.

LAO TZU

NEVER LOVE ANYONE WHO TREATS YOU LIKE YOU'RE ORDINARY.

OSCAR WILDE

PERHAPS EVERYTHING THAT FRIGHTENS
US IS, IN ITS DEEPEST ESSENCE,
SOMETHING HELPLESS THAT WANTS
OUR LOVE.

RAINER MARIA RILKE

WHAT IS A FRIEND? A SINGLE SOUL
DWELLING IN TWO BODIES.

ARISTOTLE

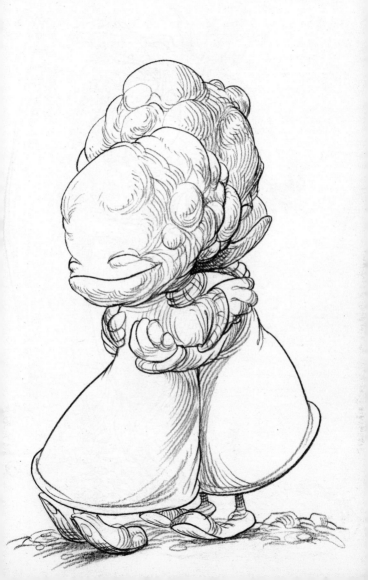

LOVE LOOKS NOT WITH THE EYES,
BUT WITH THE MIND.

WILLIAM SHAKESPEARE

EVERY HEART SINGS A SONG,
INCOMPLETE, UNTIL ANOTHER HEART
WHISPERS BACK.

PLATO

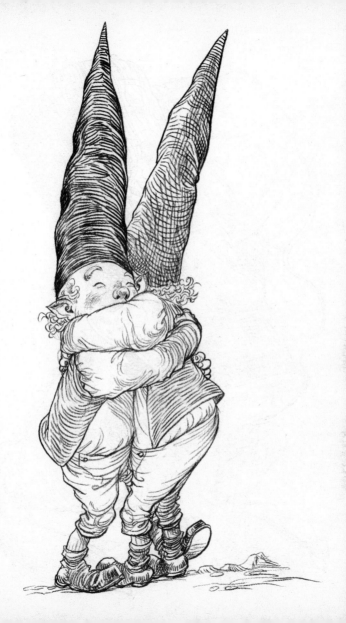

LOVE CONSISTS OF THIS: TWO SOLITUDES
THAT MEET, PROTECT AND GREET
EACH OTHER.

RAINER MARIA RILKE

About Chris Riddell

Chris Riddell, Children's Laureate 2015–2017, is an accomplished artist and political cartoonist for the Observer. His books have won many awards, including the 2001, 2004, 2016 CILIP Kate Greenaway Medals, the Nestlé Children's Book Prize and the Red House Children's Book Award. Goth Girl and the Ghost of a Mouse won the Costa Children's Book Award in 2013.

About Chris Riddell

Chris Riddell, Children's Laureate 2015–2017, is an accomplished artist and political cartoonist for the *Observer*. His books have won many awards, including the 2001, 2004, 2016 CILIP Kate Greenaway Medals, the Nestlé Children's Book Prize and the Red House Children's Book Award. *Goth Girl and the Ghost of a Mouse* won the Costa Children's Book Award in 2013.

The Goth Girl books

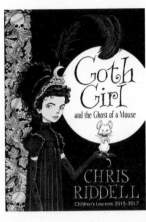

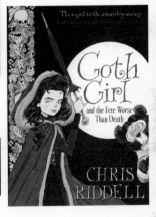

The Ottoline books

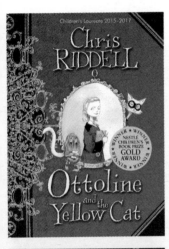

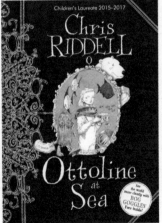

CHRIS RIDDELL'S

Doodle a Day

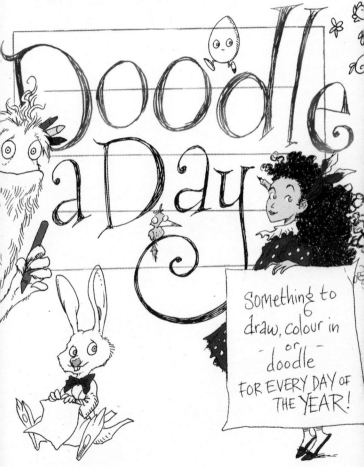

Something to draw, colour in or doodle FOR EVERY DAY OF THE YEAR!